GO DIEGO GO!

Diego's Egyptian Expedition

adapted by Emily Sollinger

illustrated by Warner McGee

Simon Spotlight/Nickelodeon
New York   London   Toronto   Sydney

Based on the TV series *Go, Diego, Go!*™ as seen on Nick Jr.®

SIMON SPOTLIGHT
An imprint of Simon & Schuster Children's Publishing Division
1230 Avenue of the Americas, New York, New York 10020
© 2009 Viacom International Inc. All rights reserved. NICK JR., *Go, Diego, Go!*, and
all related titles, logos, and characters are trademarks of Viacom International Inc.
All rights reserved, including the right of reproduction in whole or in part in any form.
SIMON SPOTLIGHT and colophon are registered trademarks of Simon & Schuster, Inc.
Manufactured in the United States of America
10 9 8 7 6 5 4 3 2
ISBN-13: 978-1-4169-6870-2
ISBN-10: 1-4169- 6870-9
0411 LAK

¡Hola! I'm Diego! I'm in the desert, in a country called Egypt. It's very far away from the rainforest. In fact, it hardly ever rains here. I came here to study the animals that live in the desert.

My friend Medina works in an Animal Rescue Center here in Egypt.
Let's say "Hi" to Medina. To say "Hi" in Arabic, we say *"Ahlan."*
Ahlan, Medina! Medina is excited to have us at her Egyptian
Animal Rescue Center.
And I'm excited to learn all about the desert animals in Egypt.

Hey! I think I hear some animals in trouble.
Do you know who is making that bleating sound?
¡Sí! They are camels, and they are telling us that
they are thirsty. It looks like the river is drying up.

BLEAT!

BLEAT!

BLEAT!

Medina is worried because camels need water in the hot desert!
How will the camels have water to drink if the river is dry? We have to find a way to get water to the camels! Medina says her friend Jamal the Camel can help. He knows everything about the desert.

Jamal says there is a magic Golden Cloud that can make it rain at any time. But no one has seen the Golden Cloud for a very long time. The Golden Cloud was hidden in one of the Great Pyramids for safekeeping.

We need to go to the pyramids to find the Golden Cloud so we can bring water to the river and save the thirsty camels!

The pyramids are across the desert. It's very hot in the desert, so Medina's mommy gave us special robes to protect us from the hot sun.

Oh, no! It looks like the hump on Jamal's back is getting saggy.

Medina says that this is what happens when camels haven't eaten enough food!

I can use my Field Journal to figure out what food we can find in the desert for Jamal to eat. My Field Journal says that camels eat thorny desert plants. They have super-thick lips, so the thorns don't hurt them.

Look! I see a thorny plant that Jamal can eat. Do you see it?
Great! Jamal feels much better now that he's had some food to eat.
Now let's get to the Great Pyramids and find the Golden Cloud! Medina's special pyramid radar says we are almost there.

Look! There are desert rocks! We've got to get over these rocks to get to the pyramids.

Medina sees scorpions on the rocks. We have to be careful not to step on them! We need to jump over the scorpions.

Jamal says he needs our help jumping over the rocks and the scorpions. Will you help us? Say "Jump! Jump!"

Hooray! We jumped over the rocks and we didn't step on the scorpions!

We're almost near the Great Pyramids, but it looks like a sandstorm is headed our way. We've got to keep going so we can find the Golden Cloud! How will we get through the storm?

Jamal says that camels have special double eyelashes that protect them in a sandstorm. Medina and I can use our hands to cover our eyes.

Wow! Sand is swirling everywhere!
It's starting to clear, and Medina sees the Great Pyramids!
Let's keep going!

There are three Great Pyramids! How will we know which one has the Golden Cloud? Jamal has a special necklace that will help us figure it out. He says if we hold it up to the sun and then point it at the pyramids, a rainbow will appear over the pyramid with the Golden Cloud.

Medina is going to point the medallion at each pyramid.
When we see a rainbow over one of the pyramids, we have to say "Rainbow!"
Do you see a rainbow? Say "Rainbow!"
Look! The rainbow is over that pyramid. That means the Golden Cloud is in there.
¡Al rescate! To the rescue!

Whoa! It looks like the entrance to the pyramid is blocked by a bunch of thorny plants. Luckily, someone with us can chew through thorny plants. Do you know who? Yeah, Jamal the Camel! Jamal can chew right through those plants so that we can get inside the pyramid! Chew! Chew! Chew!

Hooray! We made it inside the pyramid thanks to Jamal's great chewing.

The Golden Cloud is in here somewhere, but there are so many paths. How will we find the one we need? Jamal says that the path with the drawing of a cloud will lead us to the Golden Cloud. There is a lot of dust covering the drawings. We have to blow it away.

Is that a drawing of a cloud? No, it's a snake. We should keep looking for the path we need.

Look! Underneath all this dust, there's a drawing of a cloud!
Let's follow the path!

Wow! I see the Golden Cloud floating in the air! But it's too high. I can't reach it. Jamal has a great idea. He says I can climb on his back and he'll help me reach the Golden Cloud. I've got to put my arms way above my head and . . . REACH!

Hooray! I've got the Golden Cloud! Now we can go fill up the river! How can we get there really fast? Jamal says he can carry us on his back. He says that camels are very fast runners. Here we go!

I see the thirsty camels! They've been waiting for us. Jamal says we need to throw the cloud up in the air to make it rain. We did it! We made it rain. The river is overflowing with water. The camels can all take a nice, long drink. They are so happy and thankful. *¡Misión cumplida!* Rescue complete!